This edition copyright © by Wieser & Wieser, Inc.
and Richard Horner Associates, 1990.

This edition published in 1990 by Gallery Books,
an imprint of W. H. Smith Publishers, Inc.,
112 Madison Avenue, New York, NY 10016.

Gallery Books are available for bulk purchase for sales
promotions and premium use. For details write or telephone
Manager of Special Sales, W. H. Smith Publishers, Inc.,
112 Madison Avenue, New York, NY 10016. (212) 532-6600

Illustrations copyright © by Berta and Elmer Hader, 1927.

ISBN 0-8317-42682

Printed in Hong Kong

HANSEL AND GRETEL

Illustrated by

Berta & Elmer Hader

GALLERY BOOKS

HANSEL AND GRETEL

ON the edge of a great forest there once lived a poor woodchopper, with his wife and his two children —a boy named Hansel and a little girl named Gretel. They had little to bite and to sup, and the woodchopper could hardly earn their daily bread.

One night he said to his wife, "What is going to become of us? We can barely feed our poor children, and there is nothing left for us."

"I will tell you what, husband," answered his wife, "to-morrow morning we will take the children into the wood where it is very thick. We will make a fire and give them each a piece of bread. Then we will go to our work and leave them alone. They will never find the way back to the house, and we will be rid of them."

"No, wife," said her husband, "that will I not do. How could I be so cruel as to leave my children alone in the wood, where the wild beasts would get them?"

"Well, then," she replied, "we will *all* starve to death!" And she gave him no peace until he had consented. "But I am sorry for the poor children," said their father.

Hansel and Gretel had not been able to sleep because they were hungry, and they heard everything their stepmother said to their father. Gretel cried bitterly and said to Hansel, "Now it is all over with us."

"Cheer up, Gretel," said Hansel. "Don't cry, I will find a way to help us."

As soon as the parents were asleep, he got up, put on his little coat, opened the back door, and slipped out quietly. The moon was shining brightly, and the white pebbles which lay before the house glistened like pieces of silver. Hansel picked them up and put as many in the pocket of his coat as it would hold. Then he went back and said to Gretel, "Cheer up, dear little sister, and sleep sweetly; God will not forsake us," and lay down again in his bed.

Before the sun had risen, the wife came and woke the children.

She said, "Get up, lazybones, we are going into the forest to cut wood." She gave them each a piece of bread and told them it was for dinner. If they ate it now they could have nothing else. Gretel put the bread in her apron, as Hansel's pocket was full of pebbles. Then they all set out together on the road into the forest.

When they had gone a short distance, Hansel stood still and looked back at the house. He did this again and again.

His father asked, "Hansel, why do you stop and look back?"

"Oh, father," said Hansel, "I see my little white kitten sitting on the roof and saying good-by to me."

"Goose," said the wife, "that is not your kitten. It is the morning sun shining on the chimney pot." Hansel had not seen his kitten, but every now and then he took a pebble out of his pocket and dropped it on the ground.

When they had reached the middle of the forest, the father said, "Now, children, gather some kindlings, and I will build a fire, that you may not be cold." Hansel and Gretel gathered a big pile of fagots, and when the flames were burning brightly the wife said, "Lie down by the fire, you two children, and rest while we go into the forest and cut wood. When we are ready, we will come and fetch you."

Hansel and Gretel sat before the fire, and when noonday came they ate their pieces of bread. They believed their father was near, because they heard the sound of his ax. But it was not the ax, only a dry branch blown to and fro by the wind. After sitting there a long time, their eyes closed with weariness.

 When they awoke it was quite dark. Gretel began to cry. "How shall we ever get out of the wood?" Hansel comforted her. "Wait a little while until the moon is up, then we can find the way home."

When the full moon rose, Hansel took his little sister's hand and followed the track of the pebbles, which shone like silver pieces and showed them the road. At daybreak they reached their father's house. They knocked, the wife opened the door, and when she saw Hansel and Gretel she said, "You naughty children! Why did you sleep so long in the wood? We thought you were never coming home." But their father was glad to see them, for it had gone to his heart to leave them there all alone.

Not long after this there was another famine in the country, and one night the children heard their step-mother say to their father, "We have only half a loaf of bread left. When that is used up there will be nothing to eat. We must lead the children deeper  into the forest, so that they cannot find the way back. That is our only hope." Her husband wanted to share the last morsel with his children, but his wife would not agree.

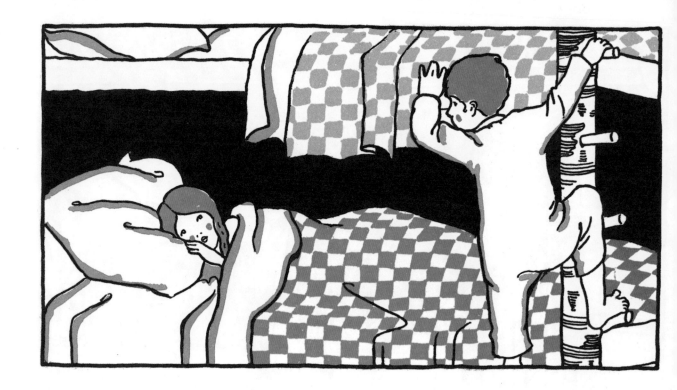

The children were awake and listening. When the parents were asleep, Hansel got up, in order to go out and pick up pebbles; but the wife had locked the door, and Hansel could not get out. Nevertheless, he comforted his little sister, saying, "Don't cry, Gretel, cheer up and go to sleep. God will help us."

Early next morning the wife came and pulled the children out of bed. She gave each a piece of bread, smaller than the time before. On the way through the wood Hansel crumbled the bread in his pocket and strewed the crumbs on the ground.

"Come along, Hansel," said his father, "what are you stopping for?"

"I see my pigeon," answered Hansel, "she is sitting on the roof, to bid me good-by."

"Silly boy," said the wife, "that is not your pigeon, but the morning sun shining on the chimney." But Hansel had only loitered to strew bread crumbs.

The wife led the children deeper into the forest than they had ever gone before. Again a big fire was kindled, and she said, "Sit down, you children, and, when you are tired, go to sleep. Your father and I will be in the forest, cutting wood, and at evening, when we are ready to go home, we will come and fetch you."

At noontide Gretel shared her bread with Hansel, as he had strewn his along the way. Then they went to

sleep, but when evening fell no one came for the poor children. They woke up in the dark night, and Hansel comforted his sister.

"Wait, Gretel, until the moon rises, then we can see the bread crumbs which I have strewn, and find the way home."

The moon rose, but they could not see the bread crumbs, for a thousand birds of wood and meadow, flying over, had picked them up.

Hansel said to Gretel, "We will surely find the road," but they did not find it. They grew very hungry, as they had nothing to eat but a few berries.

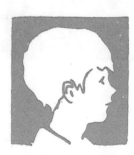

Now it was the third morning since they had left their father's house. They went deeper and deeper into the forest, and did not know which way to turn.

At midday they saw a beautiful snow-white bird sitting on a bough and singing so sweetly that they stood still to listen. The bird spread its wings and flew past them, and they followed until they spied a little house. The bird perched on its roof, and when they drew nearer they saw that the house was built of bread and butter, with a roof of cake, while the windows were clear sugar.

"We will have some of this," said Hansel, "and make a good meal. I will try a piece of the roof, and, Gretel, you take part of the window. That will be sweet."

Hansel reached up his hand and broke off a piece of the roof, while Gretel bit into the windowpane. Then they heard a voice from inside saying:

"Nibble, nibble, little mouse,
Who is nibbling at my house?"

The children answered:

"The wind, the wind,
At the window blind,"

and went on eating without troubling themselves further. Hansel, finding that the roof tasted good, broke off a large piece, while Gretel pulled out a whole round windowpane and sat down to eat it.

Suddenly the door opened and an old woman came out, leaning on a crutch. Hansel and Gretel were so startled that they let fall what they had in their hands.

The old woman nodded to them and asked, "Dear children, how did you get here? Come in and stay with me; you will have a good time."

She took them into the house, and gave them a good meal—milk and pancakes, with sirup, apples, and nuts. Two white beds were spread for them, and Hansel and Gretel lay down and thought they were in heaven.

Although the old woman had greeted them so kindly, she was really a wicked witch who lay in ambush for children, and had built the little house of good things to eat in order to tempt them away from home. When they were in her power she killed them, cooked and ate them, and then it was a feast day for her!

Early in the morning, before the children were awake, she stood beside the bed, and as she looked at their round, rosy cheeks she chuckled to herself, "How good that will taste." Then she seized Hansel with her withered hand, and dragged him into a little stable. He fought and screamed, but she fastened him in behind a grating.

Then she went to Gretel, wakened her rudely, and said, "Get up, lazybones! You must draw water and cook something good for your brother. I've put him in the stable to be fattened. As soon as he is fat enough I will eat him." Gretel wept bitterly, but she had to do what the wicked witch ordered.

Poor Hansel was given the best of everything to eat. Gretel had only crab's claws. Every morning the witch went to the stable and called, "Hansel, stretch out your finger that I may feel how fat you are." Hansel stretched out a little bone. And the witch, who could not see very well, thought it was Hansel's finger and wondered why he did not get fat any faster.

When four weeks had gone by and Hansel still remained thin, her patience was exhausted and she would wait no longer.

"Jump, Gretel," she cried to the little girl. "Run quickly and draw some water. Be Hansel fat or thin, to-morrow I will kill and cook him."

How terribly the poor little sister felt as she had to draw the water, and how the tears flowed down over her cheeks. "Dear God, help us," she prayed. "If we had been killed by the wild beasts in the wood, at least we should have perished together."

"Stop your complaining," said the witch, "there is no help for you."

Early next morning Gretel had to fill the kettle with water and put it on the fire. "First, we will do the baking," said the witch. "The oven is all ready and the dough is kneaded."

She pulled poor Gretel to the oven, over which the flames were rising. "Creep in," said the witch, "and see whether it is hot enough for us to put in the bread." She meant to shut the oven door as soon as Gretel was inside, and roast the poor child, and then she was going to eat her.

Gretel suspected this and said, "I don't know how to do it. How can I get in?"

"Stupid!" said the witch. "The opening is large enough. See how easily I could get in, myself."

She stooped down and stuck her head into the oven. Gretel gave her a push, so that she went inside, shut the oven door, and drew the bolt. She howled horribly; but Gretel ran away, and left the wicked witch to burn up, as she deserved.

Gretel ran straight to the stable and shouted, "Hansel, we are free! The old witch is killed!" Hansel sprang out the moment the door was opened, like a bird let loose from its cage. How they danced around and hugged and kissed each other with joy! Now there was nothing to fear.

They went over the witch's house, and found in every corner chests of pearls and precious stones. "These are better than pebbles," said Hansel, filling his pockets full.

"I will take some home with me, too," said Gretel, and she filled her apron. "Now let us get out of the witch's wood," said Hansel.

After they had walked for an hour or two, they came to a sheet of water. "How can we get across?" asked Hansel. "There is no boat and no bridge."

"There may be no boat," answered Gretel, "but I see a duck swimming on the water; if I ask her, she will help us over." So she called:

"Duck, little duck, here we stand,
Hansel and Gretel, on the land,
Without bridge and without boat;
Pray on your feathers let us float."

The duck swam up to them, and Hansel jumped on her back and told his sister to sit behind him. "No," answered Gretel, "that will be too heavy for the duck. She will carry us over separately."

This the good bird did. They went on happily and soon the forest began to look more and more familiar. At last they caught sight of their father's house. They

rushed up to it, burst in through the door, and fell on their father's neck. He had not spent one happy moment since he had left the children in the wood, and the cruel wife was dead.

Gretel opened her apron and the pearls and precious stones streamed down on the floor, and Hansel took handful after handful out of his pocket. All care was at an end, and they lived together in peace and happiness forever after.

From the German of
THE BROTHERS GRIMM